Amy Wild, Animal Talker

The Great Sheep Race

Diana Kimpton

Illustrated by Desideria Guicciardini

The Clamerkin Clan

Einstein

Plato

Isambard

Willow

Bun

To Cindy

First published in the UK in 2010 by Usborne Publishing Ltd., Usborne House, 83-85 Saffron Hill, London EC1N 8RT, England. www.usborne.com

Cover photograph by Peter Hasselbom

A CIP catalogue record for this book is available from the British Library.

First published in America in 2013 AE.

PB ISBN 9780794529994 ALB ISBN 9781601303103

FMAMJJASOND/16 00077/2

Printed in China.

CHAPTER ONE

"Fetch!" called Amy Wild, as she threw the stick as far as she could across the beach. Hilton, the cairn terrier, bounded after it.

Amy watched him go. Then a noise attracted her attention. She looked up into the sky and spotted a helicopter, flying across the sea toward Clamerkin Island.

"Look at that," she said, as Hilton dropped the stick at her feet. "It'll be over the harbor soon and it's getting lower all the time. I think it's going to land."

"It'll come down in the sports field," barked Hilton. "Let's go and watch." He abandoned his stick and raced off across the sand.

Amy ran after him, up the steps to the seafront and along a narrow lane. They reached the field as the helicopter hovered overhead. She could see it more clearly now and, for the first time, she noticed the red cross painted on its side.

It matched the one on the ambulance waiting in the corner of the field. A small crowd had gathered a respectful distance from the vehicle to see what was happening.

A grubby tabby cat sat beside them, gazing at the machine in the sky. "Wonderful things – helicopters," he said as Amy and Hilton walked up to him.

Any other human would have thought he was just meowing. But Amy didn't. Thanks to the magic necklace she wore around her neck, she could understand every word he said. She bent down and stroked the cat's head. "Hello, Isambard. I thought you'd be here."

The helicopter's engines roared as it came down to earth. "Just listen to all that power," Isambard shouted above the noise.

"We haven't got much choice," barked Hilton. The blast from the rotors blew his hair flat against his face and tugged at Amy's T-shirt and jeans.

As soon as the wheels touched the ground, the helicopter's engines throttled back and the rotor blades slowed. Isambard watched the machine with adoring eyes. But Amy was more interested in the stretcher being lifted from the ambulance. Lying on it was a boy with curly red hair.

Amy recognized him instantly. “It’s Tom Breck. He’s in my class.”

She waved at him. But Tom didn’t wave back. He lay motionless as the paramedics ran across the grass with the stretcher. He still didn’t move when they lifted it into the helicopter.

Tom’s mom and dad climbed in too and the crew shut the door behind them. Then the engines roared again and the helicopter lifted off. Isambard purred with delight as he watched it fly into the distance.

Amy felt more anxious. She was used to seeing Tom hurtling around the playground playing football. He looked so different on the stretcher – so quiet and pale. Was he going to be all right?

Amy still didn't know the answer to that question when she got to school the next day. She soon discovered that none of her classmates did, either.

Her teacher, Mrs. Damson, waited until everyone had sat down at their desks. Then she clapped her hands for silence. "I expect most of you know that Tom was flown to the hospital on the mainland yesterday. He hurt himself badly when he fell out of a tree."

"So that's what happened to him," said Einstein, the school cat, as he rubbed himself against Amy's legs. "Isambard told me about the helicopter."

"I thought he might," whispered Amy. Her voice was so quiet that only the white Persian cat could hear her.

Her ability to talk to animals was a secret she didn't want discovered.

"Tom's going to be fine," continued Mrs. Damson, as she pulled a large Get-Well card from her bag. "But he's broken his leg and had a nasty bump on the head, so I thought you might like to sign this to cheer him up."

Her suggestion won a chorus of approval from the class. The room went quiet for a while as the card was passed around. Then Mrs. Damson started talking again. "While you're doing that, we can decide what our class is going to do at the School Fair. Mr. Plimstone has agreed that we can give all the money we raise to the air ambulance to say thank you for helping

Tom. Now who's got some ideas?"

"We could grow plants and sell them," suggested Emma.

"That's a good suggestion," said Mrs. Damson. "But we don't have time. It's less than two weeks until the Fair."

Veronica's hand shot into the air. "We could have a raffle."

"That's boring," said Nathan, wrinkling his nose in disgust. "Let's have a stand where people pay to throw wet sponges at the teachers."

Several of the boys murmured their agreement, but Mrs. Damson looked appalled. "I don't think that's a good idea at all. And it's not the right sort of attraction. We need one with wider appeal."

"Everyone likes races," said Jade.

"It's fun trying to pick the winner," added her twin sister, Josie.

Amy looked up from signing her name on the card. "We had donkey racing at my old school's summer fair."

"That would be fun," said Veronica. "People can pay to guess which donkey will win and everyone who guesses right goes in a draw to win a great prize."

Nathan gave a scornful laugh. "Trust you girls to come up with a silly idea like that."

"There's no need to be rude," scolded Mrs. Damson. "I think Veronica's fund-raising plan is excellent."

"But donkey racing isn't," said

Nathan. "There's only one donkey on the Island. It won't be very exciting watching old Mistletoe walk around by himself."

Amy's face reddened. She should have thought of that herself. "It doesn't have to be donkeys," she argued. "We could race something else."

"I saw ferret racing on the mainland," said Luke. "Ferrets run really fast."

"Does anyone have any?" snapped Nathan.

Luke shook his head. So did everyone else. "Oh dear," said Mrs. Damson. "It looks as if the race idea won't work after all."

"Great," said Nathan. "Let's do the wet sponges."

But Amy wasn't ready to give up yet. She thought hard – surely there must be some animals on the Island that were suitable.

The idea came in a rush. "We could race sheep!" she cried. "I know where I can get some of those."

Luke grinned. "That would be great – much funnier than ferrets."

"Everyone would want to watch a sheep race," said Jade.

"They've probably never seen one before," said Josie.

"I certainly haven't," said Mrs. Damson. "Now hands up everyone who thinks Amy's idea is the best."

The class voted 14–1 in favor of the sheep race. Only Nathan thought it

was a bad idea. "Sheep are stupid," he sneered. "You'll never get them to do what you want."

Amy hoped he was wrong. If he wasn't, she would be letting everyone down.

CHAPTER TWO

As soon as school was over, Amy ran home to the Primrose Tea Room. Mom and Dad were busy serving customers, but Granty, her great-aunt, was taking a break in the kitchen.

"Can I go to visit Flora Winthrop?" Amy asked.

Granty smiled. "Of course you can. Flora always loves to see you. You did

such a good job of looking after her animals when she was away."

"I'll be back in time for supper," Amy promised. Then she found Hilton and headed up the hill toward the old lady's cottage. A border collie ran to greet them as they approached.

"Hello, Barney," said Amy. "Where's Flora? I need to talk to her."

"She's in the kitchen." He sniffed deeply as he led the way toward the cottage. "Doesn't that cooking smell good?"

Hilton agreed, but Amy's human nose wasn't as sensitive as the dogs'. She didn't smell the delicious aroma of baking until she reached the back door. But when she did, it was so good that it made her mouth water.

Flora smiled broadly when she saw Amy in the doorway. "Come in, my dear. You're just in time for one of these." She lifted a tray of muffins from the oven, popped one on a plate and pushed it across the table.

"That looks yummy," said Amy, as she sat down in front of it. She spread the warm muffin with home-made blackcurrant jam and took a bite. It tasted even better than it looked.

Hilton stared at her with hungry eyes. "My tummy's empty too," he whined.

Flora couldn't understand him, but she guessed what he wanted. "Don't

worry," she said, "I haven't forgotten you." She gave a large dog biscuit to him and another to Barney. Then she turned back to Amy and asked, "What brings you here today?"

"I need to ask a favor," Amy replied. "Can I borrow your sheep?"

Flora's eyes opened wide in surprise. "Whatever do you want them for?"

While she finished her muffin, Amy explained about Tom's accident, the School Fair and her class's plan to raise money for the air ambulance. "We want to run a sheep race," she said, as she sucked the last traces of jam from her fingers. "And we'd like to use Floss, Drum, Clover, Sprig and Tallulah."

To her dismay, Flora looked doubtful. "How are you planning to make them race?" she asked. "I hope you're not going to get your dog to chase them."

"Of course I won't," said Amy. "I'm going to rattle a bowl of food on the

other side of the finish line. They're sure to run toward that."

"That might work," said Flora. "But then again, it might not. I think we'd better try it and find out."

She brushed the flour off her hands and took off her apron. Then she led the way to the shed, where she let Amy pour a scoop of grain into a metal bowl. The sound brought three golden brown chickens scurrying from the bushes. They clucked with pleasure when they saw Amy.

"It's good to see you again," said Faith.

"But isn't it a little early for supper?" said Hope.

"I don't care," said Charity. "It's always a good time to eat."

Amy sprinkled some of the grain on the floor to keep the chickens happy. Then she set off with Flora toward the sheep field, with Hilton following close behind.

When they reached the gate, they saw the sheep spread out in the middle of the field like five woolly mounds in a sea of grass. They all had their heads down, grazing.

"Let's see if you can make them race," Flora said.

Amy shook the bowl hard so the grain rattled inside it. The sheep put their heads up. Amy shook the bowl again and all five started to run toward her.

"It works," said Amy with a big grin.

"I'm not so sure," said Flora. "Getting them started is the easy part. It's the finishing that's worrying me."

As the sheep ran across the field, they got closer and closer together. Amy expected them to jostle and shove to try to be the first to reach the food. But they didn't.

"After you, my dear," said Floss, as she slowed down to let Drum overtake her.

Drum slowed down even more. "No – after you," she bleated.

"Perhaps we should let Clover go first," suggested Tallulah. "I'm sure she's much hungrier than me."

"I was first last time," said Clover. "It's Sprig's turn. Let her through."

The first four sheep moved aside to let Sprig trot between them. Then they formed an orderly line behind her, waiting politely for their turn to eat.

Amy groaned. “That’s not going to work on the day. Don’t they understand about winning?”

“They’ve never needed to,” said Flora. “I taught them to take turns when they were lambs.”

“I remember that,” said Clover. “She could only bottle-feed us one at a time so we learned to wait in line.”

“That’s a surprise,” said Hilton. He sat down and scratched his ear. “I thought sheep never learned anything.”

Tallulah stamped her foot crossly. “That’s not true,” she bleated. “We learn very well if we’re taught correctly.”

Flora put her arm around Amy’s shoulders. “I’m sorry, my dear. The sheep race was a great idea, but it’s not going to work. You’ll have to think of something else.”

Amy hated the thought of telling her class that her plan had gone wrong. Everyone would be so disappointed – everyone except Nathan, of course.

He would love making fun of her for failing.

Then she remembered what Tallulah had just said and that gave her an idea. “I don’t want to give up yet,” she told Flora. “You managed to teach the sheep to take turns, so I should be able to teach them to run a race.”

The five sheep stared at her with puzzled expressions.

“What’s a race?” asked Clover.

Amy sighed. This was going to be harder than she had thought.

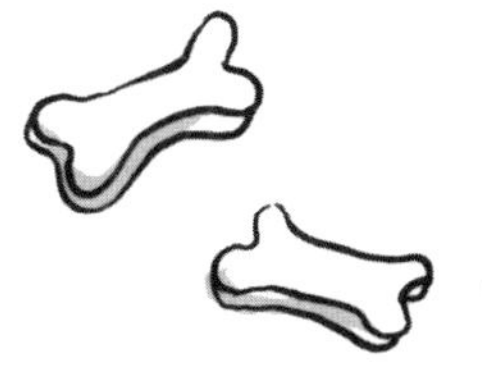

CHAPTER THREE

Flora Winthrop laughed. "I can't think how you're going to train my sheep. But you're welcome to try."

"You're going to be so proud of them," Amy promised as they walked back to the cottage. "The Great Sheep Race will be the talk of the whole Island."

"I hope that won't be because it's

gone wrong," muttered Hilton.

Amy arranged to come back the following afternoon to start the training. Then she set off for home, munching a slice of freshly baked gingerbread that Flora insisted she took with her.

"Do you know much about training sheep?" asked Hilton as he trotted along beside her.

"Nothing at all," said Amy. "I'm going to need some help from the clan."

"Brilliant," said Hilton, wagging his tail. "I love it when we've got something to do." He was the only dog in the group of animals that looked after Clamerkin Island. The rest of the clan consisted of four cats, a parrot and Amy herself.

"Tell them to meet me at Flora's at four o'clock tomorrow," said Amy.

Mrs. Damson bounced into class the next morning, full of excitement.

"I've got some wonderful news," she announced. "The air ambulance crew have organized a fantastic first prize for us – a trip in a helicopter where you get a chance to handle the controls."

"Wow," said Nathan. "I want to win that."

"So will everyone on the Island," said Veronica. "They'll all want to pick the winning sheep now."

"That's assuming the race is going ahead," said Mrs. Damson. She looked at Amy and asked, "Have we got any sheep yet?"

"Five," Amy replied proudly.

"I bet they don't know how to race," sneered Nathan.

"They will soon," said Amy, trying

to sound more confident than she felt. "Flora says I can go every afternoon and train them."

Mrs. Damson looked concerned. "That's a very big job to handle by yourself. Do you need some help?"

"No, thanks," said Amy. "I'm sure I can manage. The sheep are used to me." She didn't want any of her classmates watching her training sessions. It would make it hard to talk to the sheep without being noticed.

"Let me know if you change your mind," said her teacher. Then she turned to the class and added, "That leaves the rest of you with the job of organizing the race itself."

While she was talking, Einstein

jumped onto Amy's lap with a puzzled expression on his face. "I thought Hilton said you wanted help."

"I do," whispered Amy. "But for this job I need my animal friends, not my human ones."

The clan gathered at the sheep's field at four o'clock. Amy was the first to arrive. She had Hilton with her and Granty's parrot, Plato.

"I'm looking forward to this," he squawked. "I love watching horse racing on TV."

Isambard and Einstein arrived next, closely followed by Bun, the fat black cat from the bakery. Last was Willow – the Siamese from the post office.

She glanced around her anxiously as she slipped out from the shelter of the hedge. "Where's Barney? He likes chasing cats."

"Don't worry," said Amy. "He's promised to stay away from us so he's not tempted."

While they were talking, the sheep ambled over to see what was happening.

"This is exciting," said Sprig. "We don't usually have so many visitors."

"You'll see lots more people at the School Fair," said Amy. Then she explained about the class wanting to raise money for the air ambulance and how they'd decided to do that with a sheep race.

The explanation took longer than she'd expected because the sheep kept interrupting.

"What's a helicopter?" asked Floss.

"What's an ambulance?" asked Tallulah.

Finally, Clover repeated her question from the day before. "What's a race?"

This time Amy was prepared. "The best way to learn that is to watch one." She pointed at the four cats and continued. "My friends here are going to run a race to show you what's involved."

Bun looked appalled. "Does that include me?"

"Of course it does," said Einstein.

"The more of us the better," Willow added.

Bun's head drooped. "I'm not very good at running," he mewed.

"Maybe you'd be better if you didn't eat so much," said Isambard.

Bun pricked up his ears. "Speaking of eating, my tummy is empty. Do you think we should have a little snack before we start?"

"No!" said Willow. "Extra food will just slow us down."

"But you can have something afterwards," said Amy, pulling a plastic bag from her pocket. "There's a sardine here for each of you and an extra one for the winner."

Bun stared at the bag and licked his

lips. "What are we waiting for?" he cried. "Let's race."

Hilton led the cats halfway down the field and lined them up. Then Plato squawked, "Ready – set – go!" and the race was under way. Willow hurtled into the lead with Einstein and Isambard side by side in second place and Bun close behind.

The sheep caught the excitement. "Come on, Einstein," cheered Floss.

"You can do it, Willow," baaed Drum.

Bun was still in last place as they approached the finish line. Then Amy waved the bag of sardines in the air, and the sight of it gave the black cat new strength. He bounded forward

with an amazing burst of speed, shot past the other three and won.

The sheep bounced up and down with delight.

"That looks fun," said Tallulah.

"Can we try?" said Sprig.

Only Clover looked doubtful. "I don't think I like sardines."

Amy laughed. "You don't have to." She showed them the bowl of grain she'd gotten from the shed when she arrived. "Now follow Hilton to the far end of the field and he'll help you line up."

"That's further than we ran," said Bun.

"They're bigger than you," Amy explained. "And they'll have to run further than that in the real race – the class has already designed the track."

When the sheep were in position, Plato squawked, "Ready – set – go!" again and Amy rattled the food in

the bowl. The sheep ran toward her like they had the day before. But this time they were really racing. They galloped as fast as they could, jostling for first position instead of giving way to each other.

"Great," said Amy. But she spoke too soon. Halfway up the field, the sheep started to get tired. They slowed from a gallop to a trot and then from a trot to a walk. As they staggered across the finish line, their sides were heaving and they were gasping for breath.

"That was a long way," panted Clover.

"My legs can't run that far," puffed Tallulah.

Amy tried not to let them see how disappointed she was. They had tried so hard that it wasn't fair to criticize them. But she knew the Great Sheep Race would be a disaster if the same thing happened at the School Fair.

CHAPTER FOUR

Amy sat down by the panting sheep and wondered what to do next. While she was thinking, Plato pulled at her sleeve with his beak to attract her attention. Then he tipped his head to the side and squawked, "In the horse races on TV, the horses keep running right to the end. Are sheep races different?"

"They're not supposed to be," sighed Amy.

"I'm sorry we let you down," said Floss, hanging her head in shame.

"We don't usually do much running," said Sprig.

Willow sat down and curled her tail around her feet. "What *do* you do all day?" she asked.

"Eat, mainly," said Clover. "And when we're not eating, we chew our cud like this." She burped up a mouthful of grass she'd eaten earlier and started to chew it steadily.

Bun was impressed. "I wish I could eat my food twice. It would be double the fun and double the taste."

"And you'd probably end up double

the size," said Isambard.

Einstein licked his paw thoughtfully. "The school football team runs a lot. They do exercises to get fit."

"So does Mom," said Amy. "She goes to an exercise class at the Community Hall."

"That sounds fun," said Sprig.

"Can we go too?" asked Tallulah.

Hilton howled with laughter. "You can't do that. You're sheep."

Amy nudged him with her elbow. "Don't be rude," she whispered. "They'll get offended." Then she turned

to the sheep and said, "He only means you can't go to the class. You can do exercises up here."

Einstein nodded. "I'll watch the football team practice and show you what they do."

"We'd better start tomorrow," said Amy. "The race is only eleven days away so there's no time to waste."

The following afternoon the clan met on the road to Flora's cottage. "Did you find out about the exercises?" Amy asked Einstein.

The white cat stuck his tail in the air and looked very pleased with himself. "I watched the whole session and memorized everything," he purred as

they walked to the sheep's field.

The sheep were waiting for them by the gate. They were lying down, chewing their cud and looking very relaxed.

"We've taken it easy all day," said Sprig. "Saving our energy for you."

Amy waved the white cat forward. "Einstein's in charge this afternoon," she explained. Then she joined the rest of the clan to watch.

"Good afternoon, ladies," said Einstein in a rather nervous voice.

"Good afternoon, Einstein," bleated all five sheep together.

This slight success boosted the white cat's confidence. His voice didn't shake at all as he said, "As you're all lying down already, we'll start with some lying down exercises."

"I know how to lie down," said Floss. "I thought we were learning to run."

"If it helps the football team, it's sure to help you," said Einstein. "Now, ladies. Please roll on your backs."

The sheep leaped to their feet in alarm. "We can't do that," said Sprig. "We've got too much wool."

"We might get stuck," said Tallulah.

"I got stuck on my back once," wailed Drum. "It was very scary. I had to lie there all afternoon until Flora found me and turned me right side up."

"Calm down," said Amy. "No one's

going to make you roll over if you don't want to." She glanced at Einstein and added, "I'm sure there are lots of exercises you can do standing up."

"Loads," he replied. "Loads and loads." Then he turned back to the sheep and said, "Please stand in a line, ladies."

The sheep did as they were told.

The white cat waited until they were ready. Then he announced, "We'll now move on to arm exercises."

"They don't have arms," hissed Willow.

"Sorry, ladies," said Einstein, quickly, "I should have said foreleg exercises. Now please raise both your forelegs as high as you can."

The sheep did as they were told. Then they fell on their noses.

"I'm not feeling any fitter yet," said Sprig.

"I'm definitely less fit," Tallulah wailed, as she rubbed her bruised nose with one hoof.

Amy stepped close to Einstein and whispered, "Move on to the next exercise."

"I can't," said Einstein. His voice was shaking again, and tinged with panic. "My mind's gone blank. The only other exercises I can remember involve footballs and we don't have any."

"Does that mean it's time for a snack?" asked Bun.

"No, it doesn't!" said Isambard. He strode forward and gently nudged Einstein out of the way. "Let me try. I've watched my human do exercises."

He waited until the sheep were back on their feet before he began. "Let's do some little jumps like this." He started

to bounce gently on his paws and the sheep copied him.

He bounced higher. So did the sheep.

He bounced faster. So did the sheep.

"I like this," said Drum.

"So do I," said Tallulah. "It makes me feel tingly all over."

Isambard switched to running in place. So did the sheep.

Clover looked puzzled. "It's going to take a long time to run the race like this," she said.

"I told you sheep can't learn anything," said Hilton. "We might as well give up now."

Luckily, the tabby cat was more persistent. "Let's jog," he called and started to run slowly in a large circle.

The sheep trotted behind him, looking very happy.

"I'm nowhere near as winded as yesterday," said Sprig, when they got back to where they started.

"Neither am I," Floss agreed.

"At this rate, we'll soon be fit enough to race," said Drum.

Amy felt more confident too. There were only ten days left until the big day, but she was sure she could get the sheep ready in time now she had Isambard's help. The Great Sheep Race was going to be a huge success – provided nothing else went wrong.

CHAPTER FIVE

The next morning Mrs. Damson came into class carrying a large box. "It's the tickets for the race," she explained, as she handed out samples for everyone to see. "They're in two halves – half for the person to keep and half to go into the prize drawing if that sheep wins."

Amy thought they looked gorgeous. Each ticket had the name of one of

the sheep on it and the words "Win a helicopter ride" in large letters.

"I'm going to win that," declared Nathan.

"You'll have to be very lucky," said Veronica. "You won't even be in the prize drawing unless you sponsor the winning sheep."

Nathan gave a smug laugh. "I've already solved that problem. I'm going to buy five tickets – one for each sheep. That way I'll definitely be in the drawing."

"That's cheating," said Amy.

Nathan folded his arms and glared at her. "No, it's not."

"Yes, it is," said Mrs. Damson. "Look at the rules on the back of the ticket.

They clearly say that no one can pick more than one sheep. If you want to win the prize, you'll have to pick the sheep that wins the race."

"I'd better not enter," said Amy. "It wouldn't be fair because I know how fast they all run."

Nathan raised his eyebrows. "Of course you do," he said quietly. Then he unfolded his arms and smiled at her. "I hadn't realized that before."

Amy wasn't sure she liked his smile. It didn't seem genuine. But before she could think about it any more, Veronica changed the subject. "I like the way the tickets for each sheep are a different color," she said.

"It would be good if the sheep were

colored too," said Emma. "It would help everyone tell them apart."

"We could paint them," Jade suggested.

"Or we could dye their wool," added Josie.

Amy gulped. "I don't think Flora would let us." She was fairly sure the sheep wouldn't approve either, but she didn't mention that.

"What a pity," said Emma. "The sheep will all look the same from a distance unless we do something."

"How about ribbons?" said Amy. "I could tie colored ribbons on their heads to match their ticket colors."

She glanced at Nathan, expecting him to laugh at her suggestion as

usual. But he didn't. Instead he smiled at her again and said, "That's a really good idea."

This time Amy was sure his smile wasn't real. There was something slightly sneaky about it. What was Nathan up to?

*

The next few days whirled past. While the rest of her class put up posters and sold tickets, Amy spent all her spare time training the sheep with Isambard.

As the day of the School Fair grew closer, she found it harder and harder to concentrate on lessons. But it wasn't just the Great Sheep Race that was occupying her mind. Nathan was still behaving very strangely.

Every time she looked at him, he smiled that same peculiar smile. He let her go into lunch ahead of him instead of barging her out of the way, and he didn't make any of the snide remarks she was used to. Instead he started making comments that were

surprisingly pleasant.

"Your hair looks nice today," he said on the Monday before the Fair.

"I liked that story you wrote," he said on Tuesday.

"Congratulations on getting all your math right," he said on Wednesday.

On Thursday, Amy and Einstein retreated to the far corner of the playground to discuss the situation. "Maybe I'm wrong about his smile being sneaky," she said. "Maybe he really has changed."

"No, he hasn't," said Einstein. "He's still the same old Nathan when you're not looking. He kicked me this morning when I was waiting for you at the school gate."

"That might have been an accident," said Amy. "You do get under people's feet sometimes."

"But I didn't today. I know that kick was deliberate. He did that nasty laugh of his at the same time."

Amy bit her lip thoughtfully. If Nathan hadn't changed, why was he pretending that he had? What could he gain by being nice to her?

On Friday afternoon, Mrs. Damson abandoned normal lessons. "You're all going to help Mr. Plimstone build the track for tomorrow's race," she explained as she led the class out onto the school field.

Mr. Plimstone was waiting for them beside a huge pile of hay bales. "I've already marked the edges of the track with white paint," he announced. "Now I want you to put a line of hay bales along each side to stop the sheep from running out. We

don't want any gaps, so make sure the bales are really close together, especially at the corners."

"Can we make jumps with them too?" asked Luke. He bounded onto one of the bales and off the other side to show what he meant. "It would make the race more interesting."

Amy shook her head. "They'd confuse the sheep," she said. "They haven't practiced jumping." She turned away and tried to pick up one of the bales. It was heavier than she expected.

"Let me help," said Nathan, smiling his strange smile again. He grabbed hold of the other side of the bale and helped Amy lift it into place.

She glanced around, hoping to spot someone else to work with. But the others had already paired up. She was stuck with Nathan now.

"How are the sheep?" he asked as they lifted the next bale.

"Fine," said Amy. "They've really gotten the hang of racing, and they're much fitter than they were."

"You must know them well," said Nathan as they carried the bale toward the track. "I bet you know all the little differences between them."

"Of course I do," Amy replied. Nathan was obviously trying hard to be pleasant. Maybe she was wrong to be so suspicious of him.

They put their bale of hay down at the end of the line and pushed it up close to its neighbor. Then Nathan straightened up and said, "I bet Drum is a fast runner – much faster than the others."

Amy was about to tell him he was

wrong, when Nathan gave the bale a hard kick to see if it would move any further.

That movement reminded Amy that he'd kicked Einstein the day before. Nathan hadn't changed. This niceness was just an act, and she suddenly understood what it was all about.

"That's cheating," she yelled as she stepped away from him.

"No, it's not," said Nathan. "I'm just being friendly."

Amy put her hands on her hips and glared at him. "You can't fool me that easily. I know what you're up to."

"Oh yeah? And what's that then?" asked Nathan.

"You're trying to trick me into telling you which sheep will win, and I'm not going to fall for it."

Nathan's eyes narrowed, and his fake smile was replaced by an angry scowl. "Suit yourself," he snapped. "But somehow or other, I'm going to win that helicopter ride. Just wait and see."

CHAPTER SIX

"I'm worried," Amy told Hilton as they walked up to the sheep's field to meet Isambard. "Nathan looked very smug when we left school this afternoon. I'm sure he's thought of some other way to cheat."

"He doesn't have much time to do it," said Hilton. "The race is tomorrow afternoon."

At that moment, Amy spotted Flora waiting for them at the gate. That was a surprise. Up until now, the old lady had let her get on with the training by herself. Why had that changed today?

Flora must have spotted the uncertainty on Amy's face. "Don't worry," she said. "I just wanted to tell you that Mr. Dabbit from Cliff Farm has promised to take the sheep to the Fair in his trailer."

"That's great," said Amy. "Thanks for organizing it."

"I'm delighted to help," said Flora. She reached over the gate to tickle Clover's ears. Then she laughed. "I saw the strangest thing this morning. My

sheep were running around the field, one behind the other, following a tabby cat. If I didn't know better, I would have thought he was taking them for a jog."

Amy's heart jumped, but she tried not to panic. "That must have looked funny," she said, as calmly as she could.

"It was," said Flora. "And, of course, the whole jogging idea is quite ridiculous – they're animals, not humans."

"That's true," Amy agreed. She hoped the old lady didn't notice that Isambard had walked up behind her – it might reawaken her suspicions.

Luckily, Hilton realized the danger too. "Hide!" he barked, and the tabby cat dived for cover under a nearby bush.

"Now I must be going," said Flora.

She turned and headed back toward her cottage without seeing Isambard. "I've promised to make some of my muffins for the cake stall."

As soon as she had gone, the tabby cat crept out from his hiding place. "What's going on?" he asked.

"She saw us jogging," Clover explained.

Isambard's tail shot up in alarm. "I'm sorry. I didn't realize she was watching."

"Neither did we," bleated Tallulah.

"And there's no harm done," said Drum.

Sprig nodded her agreement. "Luckily, she didn't believe her own eyes."

Amy climbed over the gate and joined the sheep. "We've got to be more careful. We don't want anyone else seeing what we're doing." She ran her fingers along the string of glittering metal paws that hung around her throat. "If they realize we can talk to

each other, they'll start asking why. And it won't be long before the secret of the necklace isn't secret any more."

They all looked around carefully. Everything looked normal. There was no sign of Flora or anyone else. The only movement was the leaves rustling on a tree in the next field.

"Let's get started," said Amy. "We'll just do one practice race as it's your big day tomorrow."

"Please go down to the start," barked Hilton, and the sheep moved away toward the bottom of the field. Isambard bounded after them, ready to help them line up.

Amy was about to ask Hilton to go with them when suddenly she heard

a creak. She glanced around, but she couldn't see anything.

The creak came again. This time it was accompanied by another noise. It sounded like someone saying, "Oooh!"

"It's coming from over there," said Hilton, pointing his nose at the tree where the leaves had been rustling earlier. It was only then that Amy realized there wasn't any wind – something else must have made them move.

At that moment, the creaking turned into a loud crack. A huge branch snapped off and fell to the ground.

"Help!" cried a voice from the tree. "Help! Help!"

Amy and Hilton rushed to the rescue.

She had to climb over the fence that divided the two fields. But the dog dived through it, so he reached the tree first.

Hilton looked up into the leaves and howled with laughter. As soon as Amy caught up with him, she found out why. Above her head hung Nathan Ballad. A branch had caught in the back of his jeans, and he was suspended from it like a spider on a thread. But a spider would be able to help himself and Nathan couldn't. He was well and truly stuck.

"Help me!" he wailed.

Amy glared at him. "Were you spying on me?" she asked. She had other questions, too – questions she didn't dare ask. Had he seen her talking to the sheep? Was her secret safe?

"I wasn't spying," he insisted. "I was just looking."

"And what did you see?"

"Nothing," wailed Nathan. "I'd only just finished climbing up when the branch broke, and I got caught on this one on the way down."

Amy breathed a sigh of relief. It sounded as if her secret was safe. "You're lucky," she said. "You might have hurt yourself like Tom Breck."

"He'd have gotten a helicopter ride that way," muttered Hilton.

Amy ignored his comment. She didn't want Nathan to realize she could understand what the dog said. Instead she turned to leave, saying, "I'll go and get help."

"No!" begged Nathan. "I don't want anyone else to see me like this. I'll be the laughing stock of the class."

"But I can't get you down without a ladder."

"Yes, you can," he said. "Just reach up, pull me off the branch and catch me as I fall."

"You'll get squashed," warned Hilton.

Amy suspected the dog was right, and she had no intention of getting hurt just to stop Nathan from being laughed at. "That's a silly idea," she told him. "I'll get a ladder from Flora's shed."

"No!" wailed Nathan even louder than last time. "Don't leave me alone.

I'm scared." His eyes filled with tears that overflowed and trickled down his face. He tried to wipe them away with his hand, but the movement made the branch bounce dangerously.

"Stay still!" Amy ordered. She couldn't bear to see anyone so scared – not even Nathan. "I'll help you."

She reached up as high as she could and managed to catch hold of his fingers. Then she tugged gently. That bent the branch and pulled Nathan toward her. But it didn't pull him free. The branch was still firmly stuck in his jeans.

"No good," said Nathan. "Try again."

He was lower now so he was easier to

reach. Amy slid her hands one at a time along his arms until she was holding his elbows. Then she pulled again harder. The branch bent a little more. There was a noise, too – a stretching, tearing sound.

"Keep going," barked Hilton. "Something's starting to give."

Amy summoned all her strength and pulled again as hard as she could. For a moment, nothing happened at all. Then Nathan suddenly came free and plummeted toward her.

It happened so fast that there wasn't time to catch him. She staggered backward as he crashed into her.

Amy couldn't say anything at first – the fall had knocked all the breath out of her. She lay still, gasping for air. It was several seconds before she managed to ask, "Are you all right?"

"I think so," said Nathan. He rolled over and stood up slowly. Then he nodded his head and added, "Yes, I'm fine."

"I'm okay, too," said Amy, as she staggered to her feet. "Not that you seem to care." If it wasn't for her, Nathan would still be stuck in that tree. But he hadn't bothered to ask how she was or say thank you for helping him.

Hilton jumped up and licked her hand. "You've had a lucky escape," he barked. "Which is more than can be said for his jeans." He pointed his nose at Nathan's backside and howled with laughter again.

Amy started to giggle. The back of Nathan's jeans had torn all the way across and now hung down like a flap, revealing the tiny teddy bears printed all over his underpants.

"Don't laugh!" snapped Nathan, as he pulled up the torn material. "I hate being laughed at."

Amy tried to stop. But she couldn't. "It's those underpants," she said between giggles. "I didn't think you were the teddy bear type."

"I'm not," snapped Nathan. "My gran gave them to me and they were the only ones clean this morning." He looked at her hard. "You won't tell the others, will you?" he pleaded. "About the underpants and me getting stuck and me crying."

"Why shouldn't I?" said Amy, suddenly serious. "It's true."

"But they'll make fun of me – you know they will."

"Just like you make fun of other people." She stared at him with her hands on her hips. "No – I need a better reason than that not to tell."

"Like what?"

"Like you promising not to cheat any more."

Nathan looked appalled. "But that way I might not win."

"Exactly!" said Amy. "You'll have the same chance as everyone else, which is completely fair."

"And if I don't agree?"

Amy looked thoughtful. "I think I'll

start by telling Veronica and then Jade and Josie. And Luke will absolutely love this story and—"

"Okay," Nathan interrupted. "You've made your point. I promise not to cheat any more."

Amy smiled at him and held out her hand. "Let's shake on it."

Nathan didn't smile back. But he took her hand and shook it. "It's a deal," he said. Then he spun on his heel and marched away toward the town.

Amy and Hilton watched until he was safely out of sight. Then they headed back to the other field where Isambard and the sheep were waiting. To Amy's relief, nothing else went wrong with the last practice. The sheep behaved perfectly and were surprisingly relaxed about their big day tomorrow.

The sheep were less calm when Amy went to get them ready the following morning. They bounced around nervously as she brushed their woolly coats and polished their hoofs.

As a result, the grooming took longer than she expected. But it was worth the effort. By the time she had finished, all five sheep looked like fluffy clouds on legs. Their hoofs shone and every hair on their faces was brushed into place.

As a finishing touch, Amy tied on the colored ribbons that she'd brought with her. The sheep were delighted

with the big bows on their heads. They rushed to the water trough to admire their reflections.

"Red is so my color," said Floss.

"I'm not sure purple suits me," said Sprig.

“You can trade with me if you’d rather have yellow,” Tallulah offered.

“No, she can’t,” said Amy. “You have to have the colors I’ve given you because they match the colors of the tickets. If you trade, no one will know which of you is which.”

The conversation was brought to a halt by Flora’s arrival at the gate. She looked at the sheep and smiled. “Great job, Amy. They look beautiful! Now you go and have a break. I’ll see the sheep into the trailer and you can meet us at the other end.”

The School Fair was in full swing when Amy reached the field. It looked as if everyone on the Island was there,

thronging around the stalls or eating ice cream cones in the sunshine. Many of them were already heading for the track, ready to watch the race.

Amy stopped to watch a group of children busily stuffing straw into old clothes for the scarecrow-building competition. One of them was Nathan. The smile he had painted on his scarecrow's face was just as sneaky as his own.

Before Amy had time to talk to him, Veronica rushed up. "Everyone's really excited. All we need now is the sheep."

"They'll be here any minute," said Amy.

"Great," said Veronica. "We've sold lots of tickets."

"That's good," said Nathan, who had lost interest in his scarecrow and come over to join them. "You're doing an excellent job, Veronica."

"Thank you," she said, with a hint of surprise in her voice.

Nathan edged closer to her and smiled that smile again. "Are any of the sheep more popular than the others?" he asked.

"Nathan!" snapped Amy, before Veronica had a chance to reply. "Remember your promise."

Nathan stepped back. "I wasn't cheating," he argued. "I was just trying to get a little inside information."

"Which you shouldn't have!" Amy declared. "Now go away or I'll stop keeping my side of the bargain."

Nathan stuck his tongue out at her. Then he crossed his arms and marched away.

"What was all that about?" asked Veronica.

But before Amy could answer, a ball of black fur rushed toward her and slid to a halt at her feet. "The sheep are here," Bun panted, "but they won't get out of the trailer."

CHAPTER EIGHT

Amy rushed down to the racetrack and pushed her way through the crowd to reach the trailer parked close to the starting line. The back was open, but the sheep were still inside. They were huddled by the door, peering out with wide, frightened eyes.

"Thank goodness you're here," said Flora. "I don't know what's wrong

with them. They went in without any trouble."

"It's us who'll have trouble if they won't come out," said Mrs. Damson. "We'll have to give back all the ticket money if they refuse to race."

"Maybe they just need time to get used to the place," Amy suggested.

Mr. Plimstone shook his head and tapped his watch. "It's only a few minutes to the start. You need to get them out of there quickly."

Amy walked up the ramp and stepped into the trailer. "Come on. Out you come," she said.

"No!" bleated all five sheep together.

"We're scared," said Drum.

"There's a monster out there," wailed Sprig. "A long, thin monster that keeps moving."

Amy turned and looked in the same direction as the sheep. She could see the lines of hay bales that marked the track. She could see the people crowded

behind them, talking excitedly and holding their brightly-colored tickets. But she couldn't see any monsters.

She bent down so her eyes were sheep height and looked again. This time she finally spotted the problem. Someone had hung gaily-colored flags beside the starting line. They were fluttering in the breeze as if they were alive.

Amy checked that Flora, Mr. Plimstone and the rest of the crowd were too far away to hear what she was saying. Then she explained, "It's not a monster. It's just a line of flags."

“What are flags?” asked Clover.

“Pieces of cloth tied to string,” said Amy. “They’re not alive, and they definitely don’t eat sheep. Come and see for yourselves.”

She led the way down the ramp, and the sheep followed cautiously. Tallulah walked over to the flags and sniffed them. Then she gave one an experimental chew. Finally she nodded her head. “Amy’s right. They’re harmless.”

“Good,” said Floss. “Let’s race.”

A ripple of applause ran around the crowd as the sheep lined up, ready for the start. Amy took a bowl of grain and ran to the finish line. Then Mr. Plimstone shouted,

"Ready – set – go!" and the race was on.

"It's Clover in the lead," Mr. Plimstone shouted through the loudspeaker system. "Floss is close behind and Sprig and Drum are neck and neck for third place. But at the first bend, Tallulah is making up ground at the back. She's sprinting past Sprig while Drum is

catching up fast with Floss and Clover's still in front."

The sheep hurtled around the second corner at top speed. "Clover's still in the lead. But she's looking tired. She's set a fast pace, but can she keep it up? Floss is almost level with her and Tallulah's there, too."

The crowd was jumping up and

down and shouting. They waved their sponsorship tickets as they urged the sheep on.

"And at the last corner, Floss is in the lead, challenged by Tallulah. Clover has found a new burst of energy. But Sprig and Drum are trying hard as they pound up the final straight. What a finish! This could be anyone's race."

Amy could see the sheep now, galloping toward her as fast as they could. As they raced up to the finish line, she rattled the bowl again to give them extra encouragement.

"Tallulah is the winner," shouted Mr. Plimstone above the roar of the crowd. "Floss is second, followed by Sprig, Clover and Drum."

“Great job, all of you,” said Amy as she poured the food onto the ground in five neat piles – one for each sheep.

“You were fantastic,” said Isambard, who had slipped through the crowd to join her.

"It was fun," said Drum. "Even though I did come in last."

Nathan rushed up and pushed a purple ticket in front of Amy's face. "I lost," he grumbled, "and it's all your fault." He tore up the ticket in disgust and threw the pieces on the ground.

Before Amy had time to reply, Mr. Plimstone announced, "It's time for the prize drawing."

The crowd surged forward, eager to see who won. Amy and Isambard went with them, but Nathan didn't. "I'm not hanging around for that," he muttered as he stomped away.

"Trust him to be a sore loser," said Isambard.

Mr. Plimstone held up a yellow box.

"Everyone who sponsored Tallulah has a chance," he said. "And we have a very special guest to pick the winning ticket."

To Amy's delight, the guest was Tom Breck. His leg was in a cast, and he was walking with crutches. But he looked much better than when she'd seen him on the stretcher. He put his hand in the box, pulled out a ticket and read out the name on the back. "The winner of the helicopter ride is Mr. Jones from the repair shop."

"That's my human," said Isambard proudly.

Mr. Jones pushed his way through the crowd. He grinned as he shook Tom's hand.

"The trip is for two," explained Mr. Plimstone. "Who are you going to take with you?"

"I don't know," said Mr. Jones. "My wife hates flying and my son's away in the Navy." He stared thoughtfully at the sky, as if he was searching for inspiration.

Suddenly, Amy had an idea. She ran forward and tugged at Mr. Jones's sleeve to attract his attention. Then she whispered something in his ear.

Mr. Jones's grin grew even wider. He walked over to Isambard and held him up for everyone to see. "I'm going to take my cat," he announced.

Isambard looked happier than Amy had ever seen him before. "Wonderful

things – helicopters," he said.

"You're wonderful too," thought Amy.

The ride was the perfect reward for the tabby cat. His training sessions had helped make the Great Sheep Race a success.

Amy Wild, Animal Talker

Collect all of Amy's fun, fur-filled adventures!

The Secret Necklace

Amy is thrilled to discover she can talk to animals! But making friends is harder than she thought...

The Musical Mouse

There's a singing mouse at school! Can Amy find it a new home before the principal catches it?

The Mystery Cat

Amy has to track down the owners of a playful orange cat who's lost his home...and his memory.

The Furry Detectives

Things have been going missing on the Island and Amy suspects there's an animal thief at work...

The Great Sheep Race

Will Amy train the Island's sheep in time for her school fair's big fundraiser – a Great Sheep Race?

The Star-Struck Parrot

Amy gets to be an extra in a movie shot on the Island... but can she help Plato the parrot land a part too?

The Lost Treasure

An ancient ring is discovered on the Island, sparking a hunt for buried treasure...and causing chaos.

The Vanishing Cat

When one of the animals in the clan goes missing, Amy faces her biggest mystery yet...